www.tredition.de

AF197939

Sven Majunke

The Rulers of Eden

Fall of Angels - Act 1

© 2019 Sven Majunke
(www.die-herrscher-von-eden.de)

Cover and illustrations by Corina Witte – Pflanz (www.ooografik.de)

Translation by William Thomas Hildebrandt

Graphics by www.fotolia.com
Fotolia 122496094, Fotolia 127035828

Photography by Christina Rutishauser (www.lebensartdesign.ch)

Published and printed by tredition GmbH, Halenreie 40-44,

22359 Hamburg, Germany

ISBN
Paperback: 978-3-7497-0127-8
Hardcover: 978-3-7497-0128-5
e-Book: 978-3-7497-0129-2

Foreword

Dear Reader,

Thank you for your interest in reading *The Rulers of Eden*.

Looking at the world today, with all of its different religions, we find ourselves asking: "How does it all fit together?"

We hear about one God who loves everyone, but we see so much violence.

So many religions professing a love of peace, but existing in a state of war for centuries.

As different as these religions may be, many parallels can be found in their underlying principles.

In writing this book, I have allowed my imagination to roam free. The result is a story about God and man, angels, and the birth of religion on Earth.

The plot lines are based on individual parts of the Holy Bible, but are otherwise pure fiction. None of these parts appear in scripture in the way they are presented here.

The book is not intended to convey any beliefs, opinions, or judgments; it was written solely for the purpose of entertainment.

I would like to take this opportunity to express my heartfelt gratitude to all of my proofreaders, whose praise and critique sustained my motivation to keep writing.

I am especially grateful to Kathleen Lohde and Tilman Fuchs, who helped me make difficult decisions, time and time again.

Without all of your support, the project never would have made it this far. Many, many thanks for your help.

And, finally, to all of my readers: I hope you enjoy reading this book as much as I have enjoyed writing it!

Sven Majunke

"Children do not always do as their father says.

—

They do what they see their father doing."

Jesus of Nazareth

Prologue

The Fallen One

Somewhere, in a dark place lying deep beneath the Earth's surface, a creature ravaged by war sits on the shore of the Lake of Fire. Two pairs of soot-darkened wings form visibly on the creature's back, its wingtips still glowing with heat. The creature gazes down upon a closed book. A giant sea of molten lava hisses and bubbles less than a yard away. Jagged rocks hang from above.

The creature opens the book to the first page, a blank sheet of paper in what appears to be some kind of journal. The creature breaks its silence:

"You ask who we are? Throughout the ages, people have called us by many names: angels, demons, Sons of God ... many of us have even been worshiped as gods ourselves."

The angel is interrupted by a shooting plume of fire. The ground shakes. A rock breaks free from its perch above and tumbles into the molten lava.

"But really we are just one thing: servants."

The angel directs a scrutinizing glance upwards and fishes a red-hot piece of metal out of his right pocket.

He takes the piece of metal and begins writing in his journal. His fingers tremble from the pain—or perhaps fear?

"This will be my final deed. I am going to tell you how it really happened. How it all began ..."

Eden

It all began in Eden. It was the third solstice after the angels' turbulent rebellion led by Satan.

It was still dark, but the first crimson rays of sunlight were already beaming through the towering cliffs of the Buron Gor mountains. Here in the heart of Eden the summer days were long and hot. It was a place where, unlike the rest of the world, it took only minutes for the sun to emerge from behind the mountains and disperse the shadow of night. When the days drew to a close, the sun disappeared beyond the Plain of Igri—a plain stretching past the horizon and into the western reaches of the land—gone as quickly as it had appeared. Between the Plain and the mountains stood an enormous palace and the seat of God's dominion.

Gazing up at the balcony of God's Glass Palace, as it was called, a legion of angels had gathered. For though this day seemed no different than any other, God had requested that all of His servants be present for a very important proclamation.

Never before had God called a gathering of such magnitude in Eden, and though they weren't sure of the reason why, the angels could sense something momentous was at hand.

The morning's rays had yet to reach the Throne Room's checkered black-and-white marble floor.

All that could be seen was the faint light emanating from the angels standing between the gold and turquoise columns supporting a ceiling made almost entirely of glass. In less than a minute's time, the room would be bathed in light that stopped just short of the throne.

Two angels opened the double doors leading to the Throne Room, upon which three other angels entered.

At the head of the trio was Lucifer, Archangel and Protector of Truth and Justice. He had the head of a bull, complete with two horns curved frontwards. His silk cape was covered with diamonds, rubies, emeralds, sapphires, and shone brilliantly with a vast array of other precious gems in a multitude of colors. His chest was muscular, dull and gray. The rest of his body was covered by a dark black coat of fur that gave off a silvery sheen in the light. On his back were two pairs of giant wings folded together and hidden beneath his cape. His outward appearance was noticeably different from that of the other two angels.

Following close behind to Lucifer's right was Archangel Michael, Lucifer's brother and fellow Protector of Truth and Justice. The two brothers had been created in the Lake of Fire and, despite the lack of any other telling resemblance, both emitted a faint but fiery crimson light.

Following to Lucifer's left was Archangel Gabriel, Messenger and Herald of God's Word. As Lucifer strode, head held high, past the angels standing between the columns, the latter greeted him one after another with a call of "Morningstar!" before quickly assuming a humble and submissive pose, dropping to their right knee and resting their hands on their left as they brought their gaze to the ground.

The Star of the Morning himself did not so much as honor them with even a glance.

With a stern look and eyes fixed on the throne, Lucifer kept an even pace, just ahead of the first rays from the rising sun. The only sound heard was the clacking of his hooves on the marble floor.

Upon reaching the foot of the throne, Lucifer unsheathed a magnificent sword from his gold-plated belt. He placed the tip of the sword on the ground in front of him, humbly kneeling with both hands firmly clasped about the pommel, his forehead resting on his hands.

"Father. How may I serve you?" he asked, his eyes directed at the floor.

God rose from his throne and moved a few steps towards Lucifer. His folded arms carried an object wrapped in a linen cloth.

"Lucifer. Rise and come with me. I have something to show you," He said.

Together, they walked a few paces in the direction of the door leading outside onto the balcony.

There, just before the door, stood a small glass table on which God placed the bundle.

"Behold! My newest creation. I molded it myself from clay, and Igri breathed life into it on this very night."

Lucifer slid the linen slightly to one side with his finger to see what it concealed. It was a small child, the very first human being.

"I will call him Adam," the Lord exclaimed. Lucifer remained motionless. He was at a loss for words, and found it difficult to hide his disappointment. He thought to himself:

You assembled all of the angels in the middle of the night just for this? You've created beings much more glorious than this one before.

"Truly a job well done, Father," Lucifer said with no hint of excitement in his voice.

With his index finger, Lucifer slid the cloth down to the baby's navel. A razor-sharp claw emerged from the finger, as if he were a cat. Lucifer was about to make a swiping motion when the Father grabbed him by the arm, shouting: "No!"

The claw retreated into Lucifer's finger. Surprised, he turned to the Lord and exclaimed, "But all creatures bear the Mark of the Servant!"

"This one here shall not! He has been created in my image. We shall be equal to one another in our ability to make our own decisions and …"

As the Lord continued to explain, His words fell on deaf ears. Though Lucifer could make out the sounds, he understood nothing of what was said, as if it had been spoken in a different language.

"Why?" he asked, abruptly interrupting the Lord, his voice containing an audible trace of anger. A single angel kneeling by the columns risked breaking his pose of submission. His raised eyes darted, shocked, towards Michael, who was still standing at the foot of the throne, the sun at his back. Michael felt the angel's glance, shook his head, and signaled with his hand for the angel to resume his proper pose. The angel obeyed.

Lucifer registered nothing of Michael's interaction behind him. The Father gathered the child in his arms again and opened the door to the balcony.

He walked out onto the open space, followed by Lucifer, Michael, and Gabriel.

"Though I have created much, I have always felt that something was missing. And if there is anything that I have enough of, it would be servants."

As He spoke the words, He unwrapped the baby and, with His arms outstretched to the sky, He held the child over the edge of the balcony for all of the angels gathered below to see.

Cheering erupted through the millions of angels assembled, their elation stretching from the foot of the Glass Palace across the Plains of Igri and to the lands beyond.

They bowed down and prostrated themselves one after another, the action cascading as if they had practiced it many times before. From above, their devotion rippled like giant surges of waves arriving from afar to break against the walls of the Palace.

Gabriel and Michael celebrated along with the millions. Only Lucifer looked on in bewilderment.

Act 1: Adam and Eve

Igri

"I bid you to show Adam the Garden. For too long now he has seen only the inside of the Palace."

"As you wish, Master," Igri replied to the Lord. He stood up and slowly exited the Throne Room. Adam was already outside waiting for him, brimming with anticipation. Over the last five years, Adam had grown into a small boy, but not once during that time had he ever been able to feel the light of day on his skin. He spent his days laughing and playing with angels in his room at the Palace, but his favorite pastime was to stand at the window imagining the adventures awaiting him in the outside world. As soon as he had learned to speak, Adam began pestering his Father, day in and day out. And finally, Adam's day had come. For today was the day on which his big adventure into the outside world was to begin.

"Come," said Igri with a smile, extending his right hand to the boy. In his left, Igri held an ivory-colored walking stick reminiscent of a bone from some enormous animal.

Igri was the eldest among God's servants and resembled an eighty year-old human.

His body hunched forward slightly, forcing Igri to brace himself with the walking stick to keep from falling. He wore a velvet toga that was as white as the blossoms of a cherry tree. Igri's face bore wrinkles and scars, a testament to the servant's old age. It was partially covered by shoulder-length white hair and a long beard flowing down to his chest. His luminous dark brown eyes were striking, still exuding warmth and trust after all these years.

Adam grabbed Igri's hand and pulled at it excitedly, like a leashed dog surging ahead of its owner. Not once in his life had Adam ever truly run free. Nothing in the Glass Palace had ever motivated him to do so.

But as the two figures finally arrived outside, the boy released his grip on his companion's hand.

"Whoooaaaahhh!" he cried in astonishment as he peered around, marveling at the giant Palace. The sunlight reflecting off the walls made Adam squint.

"Do not look directly into the light!" Igri called to him. "Your eyes must grow accustomed to the new colors."

The boy raced back to Igri and asked: "Are you human, too?"

"No. I am but a humble servant."

"Are you an angel? Where are your wings?"

The old man bent down to Adam, revealing the outline of a smile beneath his beard.

"Angels are not the only servants of the Lord. Everything that you see here, be it with or without wings—the mountains, the trees, the wind—all of it has some special purpose."

"What is your purpose?"

"Long ago, I helped form most of Creation. The Lord would come to me and explain His ideas, and I would draw up the first draft. If He was pleased with it, He permitted me to add the colors of life and breath existence into my work."

Adam had no idea what Igri was talking about. But that didn't stop him from rifling off more and more questions. As the two talked, they left the path on the Plain and proceeded north into a spruce forest. The woods were darker, providing relief from the burning sun of the open meadows. But rays of sunlight still poked through the trees, bathing the ground in beautiful light.

All of a sudden, Adam stopped. For a brief moment he appeared lost in thought.

"What is my purpose?" he asked, looking towards the old man in anticipation.

Igri stood still and turned to face Adam, unsure for a moment of what to say. After all, the possibilities for Adam were boundless.

"Would you like to have a purpose?"

Adam nodded.

"Well then, you can help me feed the animals. Follow me. It is not far from here," he said with a smile, extending his hand again in Adam's direction.

They walked on for a time, heading deeper into the woods, until they came upon a glass building built on the slopes of Eden's eastern-lying mountains. As they entered, Adam marveled at the brightly colored wooden floor that filled the room with a certain warmth despite the lack of daylight.

A number of intricately decorated, thin white pedestals stood inside, on top of which were placed glass cases containing baby animals fast asleep. The cases were positioned so close to one another that only a very narrow pathway remained between each one, just wide enough for a single person to pass through— a veritable maze of glass.

Along the walls, white columns adorned with gold supported the weight of the ceiling. Standing between each were angels whose bodies were that of an animal. Their faint angelic glow provided the room with a small shimmer of additional light.

Adam was speechless. Full of wonderment, he ran through the pathways between the cases and stared in amazement at the creatures inside.

"Come here, Adam. Their food is here with me."

Igri, standing close to the entrance of the glass building, waved to Adam and pointed to a small box at his feet. Adam peered at the pea-sized grains contained inside.

"Take one handful of feed for each case. And you mustn't run. The floor here is far more slippery than the one in your room."

Adam scooped up a handful of feed and did as he was told, making five trips between the feed box and the glass cases. On his sixth, Adam lifted up the box, hoping to carry the rest of the feed over to the cases. The box was heavy. He puffed his cheeks and winced under the load, while Igri and the angels began to laugh and clap. Startled, Adam directed a sheepish look at the angels. But his puzzled expression quickly yielded to one of beaming joy.

Awakened by the sudden noises, the small creatures began stirring in their cases, and soon the entire room was filled with their tiny sounds.

Adam put the box down and walked over to the animals. A little black kitten nestled on its pedestal caught his eye. The kitten cuddled its head into Adam's hand and quietly started to purr.

"Can I take it out?"

Igri removed the little black cat from its case and placed it into Adam's arms.

"Be careful that it does not run off into the woods. Otherwise it may never find its way back!"

Adam rubbed the kitten's neck while the young animal licked the back of his hand. There were many other animals in the room, but feeding time was over as far as he was concerned. The kitten was the only one Adam really cared about.

"I'll call her Sola," he radiantly announced.

Igri tied a string to a small twig from the forest and passed it to Adam.

"Here. A toy for your new friend."

Adam took the scrap of wood and watched as Sola swatted at the string. Soon Adam was running around gleefully for the first time in his life—weaving in and around the glass cases, with the kitten chasing after the string.

"Please be careful! Remember, the floor is very slick!"

But Adam paid no heed to Igri's words of caution. He was enjoying watching the kitten slide around corners. Adam himself grew bolder as he bolted around the pedestals.

And suddenly, as he made a sharp turn, Adam skidded and lost his footing. As he tried to brace himself on a very thin pedestal that held a large case filled with insects, the pedestal tipped over and the case shattered on the hard wooden floor.

Beetles, worms and spiders scattered between the shards of glass, in the midst of which Adam sat and cried. He was unhurt, but frightened nevertheless. And he wasn't the only one. All of the animals screamed, roared and hissed in panic from their cases.

"Have you been injured? Are you alright?" Igri called in a panic as he rushed over to Adam. Adam nodded as he glanced up at Igri, his bloodshot eyes rimmed with tears.

"We have to tell Father about this!" he cried.

"No. Come and help me gather up the animals. There is another empty case in the back. Nice and easy, now. Everything is fine. I will clean up the shards later," the old man reassured him, wiping the tears from Adam's eyes with a small cloth. Carefully, they plucked up the insects crawling across the floor and placed them in the empty case on the other side of the room. Having finished, they left for the Palace, neither of the two uttering a single word.

Michael

"We must tell him immediately," Lucifer urged the Father as the two moved a few steps across the terrace. Michael followed them in silence. The sun had already reached its high point for the day, and it was very hot. The Father pensively turned his gaze north, to the forests.

"He is too young for such things. Give him more time, until he stands tall and firm and his arms are strong!"

"Father, with each additional day that passes without us telling the truth, the suffering grows—if he should ever discover it!"

"And how do you claim to know that?" interrupted Michael. Lucifer came to a halt and glanced at his brother with a look of disdain.

Michael was the epitome of an angel: muscular and incredibly beautiful. Two pairs of snow-white wings hung magnificently on his back. He wore a glorious suit of armor made of pleated sliver and decorated with golden runes. On his right hip, an elegant short-sword was lodged in its sheath, and on the left hung a double axe.

His eyes were red like his brother's, and he had finely-curled blonde locks accompanied by a golden halo.

While he had grown used to the scornful look from his brother, that had not always been the case.

Before the Angels' Rebellion, it had been impossible to physically tell the two brothers apart. However, Lucifer had relished the splendor of being an Archangel a little too much. He had become intoxicated with the feeling he got when the angels prostrated themselves before him in worship, with Michael following suit in order to testify that he, too, was a mere servant. Lucifer—the monster who considered himself a god—was soon called "Satan," *the adversary of God*, by the angels who were loyal to the Father. His followers believed he possessed better judgment than God. This eventually led to a rebellion among the angels, one in which both sides incurred heavy losses.

While Michael had earned the honor of standing at the right hand of the Father when the Rebellion was over, he still could do no more than follow behind Lucifer. As punishment for his arrogance, Lucifer's beautiful and resplendent features had been transformed into those of a bull—yet all of the angels continued to call him "Morningstar."

Michael, on the other hand, had not lost one bit of his glory, nor had he committed any injustice. Nevertheless, his brother looked upon Michael as if it was he himself who had started the rebellion, and had transformed into something vile as a consequence. That didn't bother Michael.

Honoring his duty and searching for past truths lent his existence a sense of purpose.

In the distance, the trio saw Adam and Igri leaving the woods. The Father turned around to face Lucifer.

"If it is indeed so that you wish to help him find the truth, then you must train him. Help him grow stronger, and make his days shorter. Tomorrow I will decide which of you two shall have the honor of teaching him the truth."

Both brothers pounded a clenched fist against their breast, a sign of humble acquiescence. Electing to take the direct route, Michael took flight from his spot on the terrace and sailed over the Palace walls, while Lucifer and the Father walked out through building.

Meanwhile in the Garden, Adam had encountered another one of God's creatures: a Turonakko who had found a place to mediate in the shadow of a massive rock at the edge of the forest. The Turonakki, a native tribe of Eden, had a physique very similar to that of humans.

Adam slowly approached the Turonakko to examine him. The meditating creature had gray skin that was covered with patchy fine white hair and many scars. Its green eyes stared back at Adam as if they were looking right through him. Most of the Turonakko's face was creased by deep wrinkles which ran from cheek to cheek and beyond. The figure sat with his legs crossed, completely motionless, in the shadow of the gigantic rock. A shiver rand down Adam's spine. He sensed something frightening about the creature. Adam touched its arm very carefully, tracing a long scar with his fingers.

"A Turonakko!" Michael called out as he suddenly appeared behind Adam, catching the young man completely by surprise.

"Michael! Must you always sneak up on people like that?! I should have hung bells around the angel's necks when I created them!" said Igri.

"Forgive me!"

Adam continued to move his fingers down the arm of the Turonakko, looking directly into its bile-green eyes. But the meditating Turonakko displayed no response at all as he continued to stare through Adam. As Adam's fingers reached the creature's upper arm, they paused at a new scar that resembled a bite mark. He picked at the raw skin with his fingernail until crimson-colored blood emerged. The creature gently took hold of Adam's hand and moved it away from its arm, its eyes still gazing off into nothingness.

Lucifer stepped closer. "He's resting, conserving his energy for the nighttime. These creatures are nocturnal. There is no better ..."

"Lucifer!", Michael interrupted. "Remember what the Father said. He is still just a child!"

Adam looked on in fascination as the creature applied firm pressure to its wound until the bleeding stopped.

"No better what?" he asked.

"Protectors!", Michael replied hastily, before Lucifer had a chance to say anything.

"The night brings nothing that should cause you any fear.

The Turonakki may look hideous, but they serve the Father just like all of us," said Michael in a soothing tone.

"We call it the 'Festival of the Moon'," added Lucifer.

"Lucifer! Be silent!" snapped Michael.

But Lucifer laughed spitefully. "Do you fancy yourself a god? You will not be the master of me, brother!" he snarled in a threatening tone.

Michael furrowed his brow, not quite certain of how to respond. He would have preferred to use force to keep Lucifer from speaking, but the young boy was here, and the Father had ordered that no force be used in Adam's presence. So he paced back and forth, helpless and exasperated.

"I know about the Festival of the Moon!" cried Adam with nervous excitement as he saw that all eyes were fixed on him in suspense. Even Igri had abandoned his friendly smile for a look of worry in his eyes—an expression that Adam had never seen before.

"There was one night that I couldn't sleep. So I looked out the window," Adam recalled. "There were drums ... loud cheers and a rumbling that sounded like thunder. I saw fire on the hills and in the forests ... and it was moving. Then I also remember such strange screams, like nothing I'd ever heard before ..."

Adam turned to Lucifer. "Tell me, Morningstar, what is the Festival of the Moon?" he asked, wide-eyed and full of anticipation, as if he were about to hear an epic tale.

Just then, the Father suddenly appeared behind Adam, with everyone noticing His presence immediately. For his part, Michael was visibly relieved that God had arrived. Only Igri was unable to hide is concern, and the worried look on his face was one the Father was all too familiar with.

Lucifer bent forward until he was face-to-face with Adam and peered at the boy with his fiery red eyes. "Unfortunately, I am not allowed to tell you any more. But I swear to you by God Almighty: When your legs are firm and your arms are strong enough, I will be your personal guardian at the Festival."

"Really? The great Morningstar will be my personal guardian?" exclaimed Adam, the joy beaming from his eyes. He could hardly believe it.

Lucifer extended two fingers to Adam. "You have my word."

The boy grabbed Lucifer's fingers, shook them and then started off jubilantly towards the Palace with Igri.

From where they stood, the Father, Lucifer and Michael watched the two walk off into the distance.

"Do you realize what you have just done?" the Father asked, turning to face Lucifer.

"I've given the boy motivation to train. Starting tomorrow, I will personally see to it that he does, Lord."

"No! Your task for today was to protect the boy. Instead, you have sewn fear and doubt."

Lucifer pointed his fingers in the direction of Adam, who was still skipping and shouting joyfully off in the distance.

"Does the boy look the least bit scared, Lord?"

"I was not talking about the boy! We have been here before. Have you already forgotten the consequences of your actions?"

Lucifer turned towards Michael and glanced at him again with contempt.

"How could I ever forget," he snarled.

"Your oath leaves me no choice. I will permit you to be Adam's guardian. As for the training, however, you have proven today that you lack one important trait required of any good teacher."

Lucifer furrowed his brow and snorted.

"That trait is patience," said the Father. "You have made the decision for me that I intended to make tomorrow. Starting then, Michael will be in charge of the training. That is final."

With these words, the Father left the two angels behind and started off after Igri and Adam.

"You should not tempt the Father," Michael cautioned his brother earnestly before flying off towards the Palace.

The Fallen One

The summer months came and went—and twelve years passed.

Adam grew into a gallant young man. Day in and day out, Michael worked to train him.

Each new day, before the first rays of sun struck the Palace, they ran with the Turonakki across the Plain of Igri and then turned north into the forest. The Turonakki had lairs and dens throughout the forests, where they could be found meditating during the daytime.

Only one Turonakko, the leader, was allowed to dine and meditate at the Palace court. His name was Mu'rok. He was the very same Turonakko that Adam had encountered on his first trip out of the Palace, an opportunity Morningstar used to get himself appointed guardian of the first human.

The Turonakki had their own language, one that neither the Father nor any of us servants understood. But Mu'rok understood every word of ours.

Each day, after his morning run, Adam fed the animals. But most of the time, he failed to make it past the cute little kitten that he had called Sola ever since their first encounter.

He had not forgotten the lesson he learned from the episode with the shattered case. But all these years later, Adam knew every pedestal and every pathway between the glass cases like the back of his hand. The 'Maze of Animals' as he called it become his second home ...

Adam

It was late afternoon when Igri walked into the Maze of Animals to find Adam and bring him back to the Palace. The sounds of stirring creatures filled the room, but one was conspicuously absent: Adam's laugh. Igri moved slowly from one case to the next, until he reached Sola's. It was empty. He drew the edges of his mouth into a gentle smile.

He found Adam asleep on the floor a few aisles away. The tiny kitten had curled up next to Adam's face with its head nestled in his hand.

Igri took a few steps closer. His walking stick clicked and clacked like wood striking wood. Noticing the sound, Sola twitched her ears before opening her heavy eyelids and yawning. She began gently licking the tip of Adam's nose, cuddling her tiny head against his cheeks.

Adam awoke, saw a smiling Igri leaning on his walking stick before him, and immediately jumped to his feet.

"Is it finally time?" he asked excitedly.

"Everyone is preparing for the Festival. I have been sent to bring you back to the Palace."

"I've waited for this, trained for it, my whole life. Please, Igri, tell me about the Festival of the Moon. Is it a celebration, a sport or …?"

"Both," said Igri with a smile, as he picked up Sola and returned her to her case.

Adam looked at him somewhat astonished.

"I don't understand why I had to wait and train for this for so long."

"You will. Soon enough, Lucifer will teach you everything that you need to know about the Festival."

"Oh come on! Just give me a little hint. Please, please, please, Igri!"

The old man turned towards Adam and placed his arm around the young man's shoulders.

"All right then. Since the dawn of Creation, we have celebrated this Festival each and every day. All creatures take part in the festivities, not just the angels and the Turonakki.

"Do they really all participate? Even Sola?"

The old man nodded in affirmation, but his smile suddenly disappeared.

"Adam, do you recall what I told you about servants?"

Adam thought for a moment and nodded.

"The wind, the trees, the mountains—everything has a purpose," continued Igri. "At the end of each day, we honor Creation. For when the Moon is at its zenith, every element of Creation has completed its task, and a new day begins. Some servants are nocturnal and can only perform their task during the Festival.

"Like the Turonakki?"

Igri nodded and opened the door that led to the forest outside.

"What happens when a servant doesn't perform his task?"

"Well now, I would not worry about such a thing. All servants desire to perform their task, and strive fervently to do so."

"But what happens if Sola is too small and it's just not possible for her to complete her task?"

The old man pondered his words for a few seconds.

"Your little Sola has never disappointed us, and has always performed her task commendably. But if any creature should ever fail, all of us would be weaker the next day. Each task performed gives us the strength we need for the following day. Do you understand? The Festival of the Moon represents a consolidation of our energy; it makes us strong. And if one servant should be unwilling to share his strength, that energy would be lost to the other servants. But you must go now. Do not keep Morningstar waiting."

Adam embraced Igri tightly and then dashed off hastily for the Palace.

A vast number of angels and Turonakki had gathered upon the Plain of Igri. Lucifer was waiting for Adam with a few animal hides.

"Are you ready? Would you like a bite to eat before the Festival?" he asked, pointing to a table standing below the balcony with an assortment of fruits and meats.

"Eating too much before running is bad for endurance. I already ate something and took it easy to digest. I'm ready!"

"My brother has taught you well. Here, put this on. The nights are much colder than the days."

Adam took the hides and put them on. He tied narrow, soft gray hide around his waist. He took the larger course, brown hide and draped it over his shoulders so that it hung down slightly past his waist. Lucifer clipped the left and right sides together with golden broaches.

Adam turned, stooped and stretched. These hides were fascinating. We was just as warm in them as he was in the Palace. He felt heavier, but was as free to move as if he were naked.

"Can I keep the hides?"

"They are yours." nodded Lucifer.

Adam looked overjoyed. He was dressed like the Turonakki.

The only difference being his skin, which was pale white, the likely result of spending too little time in the sun. His face bore the traces of much happiness, laughter already having formed small wrinkles at the corners of his blue-green eyes. His hair was blonde with fine ringlets.

Everyone was looking up at the Father, who stood observing the sun from his perch on the balcony. The sun already stood far to the West and was beginning to take on the color of twilight.

"Let the Festival begin!" the Father proclaimed. Upon hearing this, the Turonakki ran into the forests and the angels flew towards the mountains to the east.

"It is time!" said Lucifer, enveloping Adam in his powerful arms and carrying him into the air. They flew over the forests and spotted Igri, who was opening the Maze of Animals to release the little baby creatures into the outside world.

Adam waved and cheered from above, and Igri waved back. But Adam and Lucifer were flying too high for Adam to clearly see Igri's worried look.

The pair flew over the massive expanse of the Boron Gor Mountains, an endless landscape of rock and stone. The landscape was filled with many caves, and every so often one could spot barren trees whose roots had burrowed deep into the rock over the years.

The angels had congregated in a gorge, where Lucifer landed to join them.

Michael approached, handed Adam a piece of fruit, and retreated a few steps back.

"Throw!" Lucifer ordered him.

Adam examined the fruit. He'd never seen such a specimen before in his life. It resembled a coconut. It was extremely hard and black, like Morningstar's own coat of fur, and had a rough surface.

He threw the fruit to Lucifer, who had positioned himself among the other angels about two yards away. He caught the fruit with ease and threw it back to Adam with a bit more force.

"Give me a good throw!" he snarled as whispers began to spread through the rows of angels.

Adam caught the fruit and felt somewhat awkward. After all, he had no idea what he was supposed to do. He turned around to face Michael, who had likewise joined the rows of angels two yards away. Adam threw the fruit to Michael, this time with more power. Like Lucifer, Michael caught the fruit and threw it back.

"Come on! Give us a real throw!" he said softly.

Adam still didn't know what the point of the whole exercise was supposed to be. So he decided to blindly throw the fruit in a random direction as hard as he could.

He closed his eyes and, after a short windup, whipped the fruit with everything he had towards the cliffs.

It ricocheted off the rock face and flew back towards the angels, who passed the fruit to one another using their arms, feet, head and wings—as if they wanted to keep the object from touching the ground at any cost.

After being passed a few times from angel to angel, the fruit got caught in the crown of a barren tree.

As soon as this happened, all of the angels started to cheer and stomp their feet on the ground, as if their goal was to cause the mountainside to collapse.

Adam quietly thought back to the nights in which had laid awake and listened to the cries of joy accompanied by the thunderous rumbling. Though the game still wasn't fully clear to him, he was happy that he had performed his task so far.

"The Festival has begun! Get moving! Phase Two begins now!" ordered Lucifer. Quickly, the angels took off on foot for the gorge located to the Northwest.

Lucifer fetched the piece of fruit from the top of the tree and gave it to Adam.

"Throw it, run and keep moving. This is what you've been training for your whole life!"

Adam took another deep breath, started running and hurled the fruit high up in the air in the same direction. The angels bounced it back and forth with their heads and hands, but this time there were no barren trees for the fruit to get tangled in.

The only possibility Adam saw were the few roots winding their way out of the rock above the gorge.

He saw the fruit coming towards him, brought his palms together and prepared to hit it.

He struck the fruit, sending it directly towards the tangle of roots. But the roots crumbled apart on impact.

"Arrghhhhh," the angels all cried. Everyone had realized just how close that had been.

They were fast approaching the end of the gorge, and the terrain ahead of them sloped down again. The angels continued smacking the fruit back and forth, but as they reached the hillside, they simply took flight and kept the game going in midair.

Adam, too, drew closer to the steep slope, his eyes fully fixed on the fruit that was once again tracing a high arc in his direction. Without even thinking, he leaped forward—from the edge into the depths below—with both palms intertwined again, ready to strike the fruit. He hit it in free fall, launching the fruit towards the angels high above him. As he fell he noticed that the sun had already set, and that the light he had always thought to be the glow of the setting sun in fact came from Lucifer, his guardian, who was constantly close by.

Eden looked incredibly beautiful from Adam's free fall. From above, Adam heard the angels cheering again amidst the rumbling.

The ground was getting closer and closer, and Adam could make out a few Turonakki running below between galloping deer.

Suddenly, Lucifer snatched the boy up and carried him over the forest.

The light from the moon illuminated everything.

"Would you like to see your Sola again?"

Adam nodded. He was too out of breath to laugh.

They landed in the woods, at the entrance to an underground cave shrouded by the roots of a giant tree.

"Now I know why they call you Morningstar. The whole time I thought it was day. Thanks for taking me with you tonight."

Lucifer said nothing. He lit a large twig and planted it like a torch next to the entrance of the cave. Adam looked up at the mountains. He could clearly see that the angels had lit their own torches and were now returning home. It was a beautiful sight to behold, like a snake of fire slowly twisting its way up the mountain.

"Sola is in there," said Lucifer as he pointed to the mouth of the cave.

Adam walked up to the entrance and braced himself on the roots above the hole. He peered into the opening, but was unable to make out anything in the darkness.

"Sola? Are you in there?"

The response was a menacing hiss from deep within the cave.

"That's not Sola," Adam said as he turned back towards Lucifer, only to find that Morningstar was gone.

"Sola, is that you?"

Another angry hiss came from the cave. But this time, the sound was accompanied by slow steps coming towards him from within. Adam was frightened and began slowly stepping back without taking his eyes off the entrance. All of a sudden, two yellow eyes emerged from the darkness, glaring at him. Adam slowly recognized whiskers and a set of ears flattened along the back of the creature's head. The thing creeping in Adam's direction was anything but a cute little kitten: It was a full-grown feline, slightly larger than a puma. As he moved backwards, Adam tripped over a root and fell onto his back.

"I don't understand. How can that be? Is that you, Sola?" he whispered as the hissing animal continued to slink in his direction, its eyes firmly fixed on the young man. Its tail whipped back and forth in a frenzy.

By now, the animal stood very close to Adam and sniffed up and down his left arm, the same one to which he had always tied Sola's toy: the stick and string.

The tail ceased its rapid motion and stood upright, as did the animal's ears. Adam looked it right in the eye.

"Sola, is that really you?" he whispered again. The animal bent gently towards Adam, and began licking his nose while purring quietly. Adam knew without a doubt: This was Sola.

He couldn't explain why she was so big, but he didn't care. He was simply happy to be with his best friend again. He knelt down and rubbed her head. He slid his other hand along her mouth, passing over Sola's two protruding fangs, which were now sharp and pointy. Adam cut one of his fingers, and a few drops of blood fell to the ground. Startled, he pulled his hand away and looked at his bleeding finger. He applied firm pressure to the cut with his other hand as Sola retreated into her lair.

And all at once, he heard other familiar sounds emanating from the cave.

Adam glanced up at the moon. It was nearly at its highest point. There was no longer any sign of the angels in the mountains. He noticed how still everything around him had become.

After a brief moment, Sola reemerged from the cave. In her mouth was a tiny black kitten, which she held by the scruff and now gently laid in the palm of Adam's hand.

The kitten was much smaller than the baby animals Adam was familiar with from the Maze. The tiny creature's eyes were still closed; it's fur was fuzzy and moist.

Sola carefully licked the kitten, who balled itself up and promptly fell asleep in Adam's hand. A tear fell down Adam's cheek. It was the most beautiful thing he had ever experienced.

Without warning, Sola leapt to her feet and snarled ferociously in Adam's direction. Adam realized that Lucifer was standing behind him again, accompanied this time by nothing more than a very faint angelic glow.

"Look at this, Lucifer. It's my new friend. I'll call her Takira," Adam called out to him, as Sola's snarling and hissing grew more and more menacing.

"Now!" Lucifer shouted as he ran past Adam, whom he ignored completely.

Adam turned back to face Sola. As he did so, Mu'rok jumped out of the tree branches next to the cave, brandishing a spear fashioned from a sharpened stick. Mu'rok drove the weapon through the middle of Sola's spine, deep into the ground. His face and entire body were drenched in blood. Sola rattled out a final cry before her lifeless body fell limp.

"NOOOOOOOO!!!", Adam screamed as he rushed over to Sola. But before he could reach her, Lucifer had grabbed him and flown away from the cave.

"Sola has performed her task. You should be glad. There is no greater honor."

"What? I don't understand!" Why?" Adam snapped at him.

"Where do you think the hides come from that have kept you warm tonight? Or the meat that you eat every morning and night with your fruit? Have you ever seen a tree with meat or hides growing on it?"

Adam looked down at the woods below, full of the corpses of full-grown animals, all of which had already been gutted by the Turonakki. A few angels carried the animals' young to Igri's Maze in the hills, while others transported the hides by air to the Palace.

"Now do you understand?"

"How? Why?" cried Adam plaintively.

"It is very simple. The daylight helps the animals grow, much faster than you or I. It is the reason why we keep them in the Maze of Animals during the day and limit their exposure to light. As soon as it gets dark out, we release them and allow them to grow and reproduce. We then honor Creation by hunting them and taking what we need to live. Sola's hide and flesh were the sole reason for Sola's existence on this day. Tomorrow, the creature sleeping right there in your hand will be your new Sola.

Lucifer touched down in front of the Palace, where Michael stood waiting for them. Carefully, he took the tiny kitten in his hand and, without saying a word, ran off towards the forest.

"Now stop crying and come with me. It is time to eat!" Lucifer shouted.

Igri

It was the dawn of a new morning. The first rays of light were already bathing the walls of the Glass Palace in sun. Adam, however, was nowhere to be found. He wasn't in his room and he didn't show up for his morning run with Michael. Everyone was very worried.

But for Igri, there was only one place that Adam could be. Quietly, he opened the door to the Maze of Animals, where Adam stood amidst the glass cases, gently petting the coat of a gray wolf cub and unaware that he was being watched.

The old man's mouth curled into a soft smile. No one had believed that Adam would recover this quickly from his shock. And yet, it seemed that he had already found a new friend.

But why did he look so grave? His face bore no trace of joy or any other expression. Adam slowly slid his fingers over the young wolf's coat before pulling his hand out of the case to gently stroke the hide he wore around his waist. He took off the hide, letting it fall to the ground. He then moved on to the next case, searching for something.

"Adam, you must eat something!"

The words startled Adam, but he managed not to show it.

"I'm not hungry."

"Come with me. If you don't eat, you will quickly lose strength."

Adam sighed for a moment before acceding and taking Igri's hand. The two returned to the Palace, where a magnificent buffet of various meats, fruits and hot soups had been laid out below the balcony.

Adam sat down to the right of the Father. Igri's seat was next to Adam, with Lucifer, Michael and Mu'rok sitting across from them and the other Archangels seated all around the table.

Igri brought Adam a small golden dish full of soup and sat down. But Adam merely picked at his soup, with a visibly wary expression on his face.

"Who ... what is this?" he asked as he looked at the Father.

Lucifer began to laugh.

"Ha! The boy thinks we would serve him his best friend for breakfast. Of course, the truth is not that cruel. I have already ordered Sola for myself," Lucifer said with amusement as he took a generous bite of his meal. Appalled, Adam sprang to his feet and dashed into the Palace.

The Father also rose to his feet.

"Lucifer, your task of teaching Adam is officially over! In the future, you shall keep your distance from him and never speak to him again. Is that clear?"

Lucifer snorted, nodded and rapped his chest with a clenched fist as a sign of humble acceptance. He then got up, as did his brother Michael, and the two left the table.

"Come, Igri. You must assist me," said the Father. The two men started after Adam into the Palace.

Once inside, they found Adam cowering in his room, crying in a corner near the window.

"I'm too old to cry," he sniffed as his wiped away a tear. Igri sat down beside him. Adam's unnerved state troubled him.

"One can be too old for many things. But never too old to grieve!" the old man said as he looked directly into Adam's eyes. Adam, too, noticed a tear rolling down Igri's cheek.

Without speaking, the Father approached the window and looked out, expressionless. Outside, two angels began to sing. They sang about the splendor and magnificence of God. About Creation, His victories and all that He had already achieved. But the glorious words were embedded in somber melodies. The singing angels, Servants of Praise, rendered a two-fold service to the Lord:

They proclaimed a message in the form of words while also using melodies and rhythm to express feeling.

Adam, Igri and the Father paused to listened to the angelic song.

But the lyrics about the glory and greatness of God were no consolation to the boy.

"She was my best friend. She was all that I've ever loved. And now my eyes have been opened. Over and over again, I see the image of her impaled on Mu'rok's spear. Tell me, oh great and glorious Father: How long is eternity? Where do we go from here?"

God pondered in silence as he focused his gaze on the boy.

Igri wiped another tear from Adam's cheek and looked into his eyes. "Adam, listen to me. You are still so young. Eden is a massive place, and so far you have only seen the Palace Gardens. There are still countless wonderful things to discover!"

Adam angrily seized the old man's hand, jerking it away from his face. Gruffly he said:

"I don't want to discover countless wonderful things! Sola was everything to me. I wanted to spend eternity with her. They tell me that I'm supposed to be happy that she served her purpose, but the truth is, I wish that she were still alive, and that the spear had hit me instead."

The Father extended Adam His hand.

"Come. Perhaps there is some way of prolonging Sola's life. Has anyone ever told you the story of the Tower of Arsinor?"

Adam shook his head and took God's hand.

God led the boy out his room and into a chamber across the hall, as Igri followed close behind.

The entire south wall was made of glass, and offered its occupants a magnificent view of a mountain, on whose steep slope a water fall fell into a small lake. Behind the mountain, an enormous white tower was visible with what appeared to be a round platform on top supporting a giant golden cauldron. Green and red victory banners with golden angelic symbols hung down from the platform.

God and Adam stopped at the room's south side, directly in front of the window.

"Arsinor was a second-degree angel, in other words, an angel who serves another angel. He ruled over time and space and constructed that tower to see into the future. His last master was Lucifer. Together they rebelled against me, but they lost the war and Arsinor disappeared without a trace."

As the Father spoke these words, his expression grew increasingly pensive. Adam suddenly realized that Igri was standing behind him, also staring at the top of the tower.

"This tower is his legacy, and we use it to give new creatures their assigned lifespan," he proceeded to explain.

"What happened to Arsinor?" Adam inquired, looking at Igri wide-eyed like he had when he was a child.

The old man braced himself on his walking stick and stroked his beard as he contemplated what to say.

"Before he disappeared, the Bell of Time rang five times. Arsinor was an angel, a servant for eternity.

I doubt that the ringing caused him to age any more quickly ..."

Adam did not understand.

"What I meant was: Where is he now?" he interrupted.

"That, we do not know! It is possible that he still resides among us here in Eden. That the animals age more slowly for him than for us, perhaps taking even hundreds of years before they finishing performing their service. Maybe he is standing right here in this very room, but our eyes can only see servants in our dimension of time and space."

"It is equally possible that Lucifer betrayed and destroyed him" countered the Father. He looked away from the tower, turning toward Adam.

"Lucifer is the last angel to have seen Arsinor. He refused to tell us what had happened, and for that he was punished.

If Igri's thinking is correct, then we should be able to use the Bell of Time to match your lifespan, Adam, with that of your friend. However, we are not exactly certain of what this would mean for you. You may ultimately end up inhabiting the same time dimension as Arsinor. Arsinor still serves me. He can take care of you while you enjoy your life with Sola and all of my other creations. I should note, however, that he would be the only servant that you could still see and hear. From my point of view, and from that of all the other servants, you will have simply vanished—and we would be gone for you."

"And what happens if Igri is wrong and Arsinor actually was destroyed by Lucifer?" Adam asked. Igri laid his hand on Adam's shoulder and said gravely:

"Then you would be alone on the other side, and it would no longer be possible for any one of us to help you. In order to survive, you and you alone would be forced to hunt and eviscerate the servants whom you have loved and cared for all these years. Would you be able to do that?"

"No. Not at all," sighed Adam, before turning and exiting the room. The Father and Igri followed him.

Back in his own chambers, Adam was still troubled.

"Leave me alone! You don't understand– I'll never be able to love another servant again. How could I?

Waking up every morning and asking myself: 'Is today the day that this or that servant will be called to serve its purpose and be taken from me again? Sola may have been created to serve, but it wasn't her service that made me happy."

Igri and the Father exchanged a bewildered glance. The very same thought occurred to both of them.

The old man smiled as he approached Adam, who was now sitting below the window.

"Whether you believe it or not, Adam, you are more like your Father than we had previously believed."

Adam looked up at the Father, who was still standing at the door.

The Father returned Adam's glance somberly.

"I understand you better than you know," God said. I have created everything you see here, and much more. And it was good, and was in accordance with my conceptions and desires. But despite this, I could never escape the feeling that something was still missing. That is why I created Igri, the Master of Creation. He created one angel after another, and exceeded even my boldest visions and ideas. But the feeling did not subside. I had everything I had ever desired and dreamed of, and I still felt like a stranger in my own land. The angels, Igri, and all of my creatures served me as well as they possibly could have, but as the number of them serving me together increased, the more I felt alone."

Adam fell silent. Could it really be that Glorious God, the Great Creator, felt just as lost as Adam did at this very moment?

"What ended Your grief and drove away your loneliness?"

"You." replied Igri with a smile, wiping yet another tear from Adam's eyes.

Adam stared into Igri's dark brown eyes, which exuded a reassuring warmth.

"Igri is right," the Father continued. "When I tell a servant: 'Sing!' he sings. When I tell him 'Hop about on one leg!' he hops. The angels only do what I order them to do. The result is that my needs are taken care of, but there are never any surprises. That all changed with you! Your first attempts at speaking, watching you play, trying to take your first steps—none of that happened by my command. I could not fall asleep at night, for there was such great excitement in watching you, wondering what you might do the next day ... The spontaneity in doing whatever came to your mind—and simply observing you in the process— have lent eternity a feeling of newness that had been missing here for some time."

Igri stood up, walked over to the Father, and leaned on his walking stick.

"Lord, I have an idea. Do you still have Adam's rib?"

The Lord nodded, and the two men left the room. When they were far enough away that Adam could no longer hear them, the Lord said: "It is stored in the Tower, with all other Essences of Life. What exactly are you planning to do?"

"If it pleases You, I would like to create a companion for him. And as soon as I have finished, I will return the rib to the Tower.

Azrael

"Do you still remember me?"

Adam squinted towards the door of his room. An Angel surrounded by a blinding light-yellow glow stood in the doorway. The only thing Adam could make out were the two pairs of giant white wings attached to a very thin body of only moderate height.

"No, I can't see your face. But I'm sure you're a very important angel the Father to try and comfort me," he replied, turning back towards the window.

"My name is Azrael. Before you left the Palace, we played and laughed together each and every day. Do your really not remember?" said Azrael as he walked slowly towards Adam.

Adam glanced only briefly upon the angel's face.

"Listen, Azrael. For two days, the Father has been sending one angel after another in here to look after me. I've had just about enough.

He looked out the window again and continued:

"I've said all I have to say. I've started eating fruit again, and I'm not going to starve. What else does He want from me? Should I feed the animals every morning as if that nothing ever happened?"

"He misses your laughter. We all miss it."

"Really? Who are you and what is your task?" Adam said, turning to eye Azrael suspiciously.

"You're right. I am merely a second-degree servant. I serve Michael. I am neither a suitable guardian, nor do I possess a talent for instruction. The solace I am able to provide is my only purpose. The Lord created me at the end of the Angels' Rebellion—a gruesome war between angels, one that demanded great sacrifice from Igri more than anyone. He appeared to have lost his creativity and love of detail. It was my task to comfort him."

Adam continued to watch the angel as he spoke.

He did look like one of the younger angels. Judging by his stature, he could hardly have much been older than Adam himself. Azrael had a clean, fresh face and a constant look of contemplation; any trace of a smile had long since disappeared. A sign that while the angel may not have personally experienced trying times, he had definitely heard many disturbing things.

His pale blue eyes radiated no warmth at all. Adam could scarcely believe that this angel's specialty was in giving comfort.

"If the Lord hadn't sent you to me, where would you be now? What would you be doing?"

"I go wherever the Lord's will leads me. I do whatever His will demands of me."

"You said that all of you miss my laugh."

Azrael responded with a nod.

"Is that really true? Would any of you miss my laugh had it not been a command from the Lord?"

Azrael was at a loss for words. He looked at Adam silently and pensively, his face indicating that he did not understand, and Adam simply stared back.

"That's what I thought. Though your words are supposed to comfort me, I know that no one chooses to come here on their own and give me sympathy as I grieve."

"Then I should leave now," the angel said before walking slowly to the door and opening it.

"Azrael, wait."

Azrael stopped with his hand on the door and silently turned around with a questioning look.

"You mentioned the Angels' Rebellion. The Father already told me about Arsinor and his tower. But what does Igri have to do with it?"

The angel pondered briefly, then closed the door.

"If I tell you the story, will you promise that you won't say a word about it to anyone else?"

Adam nodded.

"It all happened a very long time ago. You must not speak of it to anyone, especially not Igri. I do not wish to reopen old wounds."

"I promise."

Adam held out his hand to the angel, looking at him with eyes as big as saucers, like a child about to hear an exciting story.

Azrael clasped Adam's hand, seated himself across from him and looked directly into the young man's eyes.

"Many, many years ago, before God had even created the animals you know from the Maze, He and Igri created an entire civilization of giant lizards that thrived under the sun. They were enormous, standing several yards tall. Some could easily reach the leaves of the highest treetops to eat, and yet others preyed on these vegetarians. Back then, the Festival of the Moon was a completely different event from the one we know today. It was far more dangerous and difficult.

The angels' task was to preserve the balance. And they did an excellent job! No one went hungry, and the meat eaters were never overpopulated," Azrael recounted.

"But they were too preoccupied to notice the threat lurking among their own kind: Lucifer. He was always extremely temperamental, and constantly found ways to get what he wanted, even when his will did not coincide with the will of our Lord. This was all compounded by the fact that he was an incredibly beautiful angel."

Azrael could see the surprise on Adam's face. "Indeed, he and Michael are twins, and there was a time when Lucifer looked exactly like his brother. He persuaded more and more angels to join him, and so they too took part in killing the mammoth beings to secretly fashion weapons from their bones, and armor from their skin. These weapons were as light as wood and harder than steel. The armor weighed no more than fur, but were tough enough to smash ordinary weapons on impact. By the time the Lord recognized the threat, it was almost too late. There was a tremendous battle with huge losses suffered by both sides. Lucifer—whom the angels loyal to God called Satan—praised himself as the 'better God' and saw victory within close reach. He finally faced his own brother in battle atop the Tower of Arsinor."

Azrael paused briefly before continuing with the story:

"Igri could no longer bear all of the bloodshed, and after thinking it over, made what was likely the most difficult decision of his life: He destroyed his own creation. The coats of armor rotted away, and the weapons broke to pieces under the blades of God's loyal angels. The angels still sing songs to celebrate the courage of Michael, who opposed his very own brother, defeating him on the Tower of Arsinor. But it was Igri's sacrifice that deprived Satan and his servants of their swords. The vast plain in the western reaches of Eden was named in honor of his selfless act. The bone which Igri uses for support is only relic left of those times.

Adam remained still for a moment. There was a knock on the door, but he ignored it.

"It makes sense to me why Igri wanted a different task after all that. What did you do to make him forget the pain?"

"Forget? No, it is impossible to forget something like that, but ..."

The angel was interrupted by yet another knock, as Igri's voice called from outside: "Adam, may I enter? I have someone who would like to meet you."

Azrael rose to his feet and the signs of a faint smile could finally be seen on his face. He opened the door and winked at Adam.

Igri slowly stepped through the doorway. Holding his hand was a young woman who hid herself behind the old man.

"Allow me to introduce ... Eve!"

Ever so gently, he prompted her out into the open. Carefully, and with a somewhat shy look on her face, Eve emerged from behind Igri, stopping in front of the old man. She was a woman of exquisite beauty, roughly equal in age to Adam.

She glanced back at Igri for a brief moment, who nodded encouragingly towards Adam. Adam couldn't take his eyes off her. He simply stood there speechless with his mouth wide open.

She was radiant. Her skin was as fair as Adam's, and she had blue eyes, the shapely figure of a woman, and long blonde hair woven back into a braid that shone gold in the bright yellowish glow emanating from Azrael.

"Who is this?" Adam asked, dumbfounded, keeping his gaze locked on Eve.

"She is like you. Not a servant, but a human. Free to think and act. Do you like her?" Igri answered with a smile.

Adam was so amazed that he couldn't find his words. He simply nodded.

Eve smiled, looking at him sheepishly before taking a few steps forwards.

Adam returned her smile, even if the expression seemed somewhat forced.

"Why don't you show Eve the Gardens? She's very curious and has not yet seen anything outside of the Palace," Igri said to the boy with a wink.

The young woman extended her hand, which Adam took hold of as the two headed out of the Palace. Azrael and Igri strolled out onto the balcony and watched the pair as they slowly made their way northeast, into the forest.

"You have outdone yourself, Master of Creation! It looks to me as if in his amazement, he has forgotten all of the pain."

"I had a good teacher," said Igri, smiling at Azrael. "She will be good for him. There is only one antidote to loneliness."

"Do you think he'll ever fully get over what happened?"

"Why not?" the old man said with a chuckle as he looked toward the forest in which his two creatures had disappeared.

"Where do you suppose they are going now?"

"To the Maze of the Animals," replied Azrael. "I will follow them to make sure no old wounds are reopened."

With that he took flight from the balcony, heading towards the woods. When he landed at the Maze, he carefully opened the entrance but couldn't find Adam and Eve anywhere.

Even the angels whose glow provided the room with extra light had seen no sign of the pair.

Outside in the forest Azrael called loudly for the two, but there was no answer. No response, not a laugh or even the slightest noise. He flew over the trees and the mountains, calling for them again and again, until nightfall began closing in. It was as if Adam and Eve had fallen off the face of Eden. The Festival of the Moon would soon begin, and the proverbial 'apples of the Father's eye' had disappeared—and could be in danger.

Chills ran down Azrael's spine at the very notion, and he became frightened. Azrael flew back to the Glass Palace as quickly as he could to tell the Father he had failed his mission.

The Father laughed heartily from his seat on the throne.

"Has Adam truly succeeded in outrunning an angel? Every day he surprises me with something new!"

Azrael knelt before the throne submissively, his head tilted towards the floor. He did not dare look the Father in the eye.

"Forgive me, Lord! I know that I am not a worthy guardian."

Lucifer knelt alongside Azrael, resting on his magnificent sword in the familiar pose of submission. But his fiery red eyes remained glued to God on His throne.

"We must double the number of guardians, Lord" Lucifer said in a grave tone.

Laughing, the Father got up and approached the two angels.

"Rise! There is nothing to forgive. It is likely that the young humans simply wanted to some time to themselves."

The two angels stood up, with Lucifer returning his sword to the sheath on his belt. He turned his eyes towards the entry to the balcony, just as Michael came flying in slightly out of breath.

"Their tracks end at the eastern mountains. Then nothing. No one has seen them: No angels or Turonakko!

By now, they could be anywhere!"

"Remarkable, is it not?" the Father laughed. The angels didn't know what to make of his reaction.

"Lord! What about the Festival of the Moon? Is it not too dangerous for them to be out there all alone?" asked Michael.

"Adam knows the dangers of the Festival. Perhaps he intends to impress his new friend? Let the Festival proceed as usual.

They are in no danger. After all, they managed to slip through the hands of guardians and hunters. I think they will be able to avoid the full-grown animals as well."

"Nevertheless, Lord, should we not search for them? You stated that you miss the laughter. What will please You if they are to be gone for some time?" Azrael objected.

"Let us give them a taste of freedom, and they will return sooner or later. Aside from that, I have ordered Igri to create even more humans."

"Did I hear that correctly??" Lucifer blurted out furiously. "Even more humans? We are having enough trouble keeping the existing two under control!"

Azrael gave Michael a shocked look.

Michael simply stared back at him before briefly shaking his head and motioning for Azrael to take a few steps back.

"Keep them under control? What ever are you afraid of, Lucifer" the Father asked inquisitively.

"Lord, I was created to speak the truth. Before the Festival of the Moon I had warned You about the harm it would inflict upon Adam. You refused to listen to me, and the sorrow materialized."

"You were not without a hand in his sorrow, brother!" interjected Michael.

Lucifer stared at him with disdain.

"That piece of truth was painful! Had you yourself been his guardian, you would not have been able to alleviate, let alone prevent, his suffering."

"That is impossible to judge, but ..."

"Learn from Your mistakes!" an enraged Morningstar barked at his Father, completely ignoring his brother. "Refuse my advice one more time, and Eden will be filled with lamentations, for all of eternity!"

Michael stepped between the Father and Lucifer's angry gaze.

"Lucifer, you are getting carried away!"

God carefully pushed Michael aside and said: "No, Michael. Let him finish. I wish to hear everyone's point of view. In your opinion, Lucifer, what would you have me do?"

Lucifer moved a few steps closer to the Father, raising his index finger to his chest. A razor-sharp claw slid out.

"Lord, let me give them the Mark of the Servant. The first two, and any others that Igri creates from now on. Hardly anything will change. Then all human thinking and volition will be based on Your will. When You want them to sing, they will sing. If You want them to feed the animals and laugh, they will do it. They will never run off without Your approval. You will be happy, and Eden will be forever safe."

A serious and pensive look crept over the Father's face.

"The Mark of the Servant would change everything. It would ruin the concept of human free will."

"And what happens if the humans one day decide to destroy Eden?"

"Why should they ever do that? This is their home."

Without warning, an infuriated Lucifer drew his sword out of its sheath and pointed it at God.

"There was once a time when You valued truth. But Your affinity for these humans has rendered you weak and blind!"

Without hesitation, Michael drew his own sword and double axe as he stepped quietly, yet resolutely in front of the Father. He peered at Lucifer menacingly.

"That will not be necessary, brother. I resign my position. When You all have come to your senses, You will find me at the Lake of Fire. I want no part of the pain and suffering that lies ahead."

With that, Morningstar dropped his sword at Michael's feet and strode angrily out of the room.

Michael, visibly upset by his brother's reaction, wanted to stop him from leaving, but the Father gently held him back.

"Let him go, Michael!" If he stays for a time at the Lake of Fire, the humans will be safe. That is all that matters."

"But, my Lord, he has just openly defied you! We have already underestimated Satan's influence once, and nearly lost the war because of it. I do not wish to make the same mistake again."

The Lord nodded in agreement, his face revealing deep concern.

"That is why you shall keep watch over him. I hereby place you in command of the Guardian Angels. The mountains contain a vast amount of hidden caves, all of which lead to the Lake of Fire.

Assign the angels in shifts to stand watch at each cave, day and night, and make sure that Lucifer does not come into contact with the humans."

"Who will watch over the humans then, Lord?" asked Azrael.

"There is no danger in Eden during the day, provided that Lucifer remains at the Lake of Fire. The Turonakki can handle the guard posts during the Festival."

"As you wish, Lord!" the two angels shouted as they humbly pounded a clenched fist against their chest before exiting the Throne Room to attend to their new task.

The Fallen One

Two weeks passed without any trace of Adam or Eve. But that didn't seem to worry the occupants of Eden.

Lucifer spent his time at the Lake of Fire, watched day and night by the Guardian Angels under the command of Michael, who came to visit Lucifer daily.

Rumor spread that despite all that had transpired, Michael still cared deeply for his brother. Each day he urged Lucifer to swallow his pride and submit to God's will. But for his part, Lucifer implored Michael to call the sentries off of their mountain posts and reassign them to the humans, in particular Adam and Eve, for the sake of averting disaster while there was still time.

There was no sign of any disaster, though.

Igri created a host of new humans in a wide variety of ages and with different eye, skin and hair colors—and always in pairs.

The new arrivals received instruction from Azrael and the Turonakki. None of the new humans experienced the same agony as Adam had when they took care of the animals; instead, they all saw it as part of a natural cycle.

It wasn't long before the number of humans in Eden began to surge, and as it did, large swaths of the Plain of Igri were cultivated to feed the burgeoning population. Igri was ordered to design creatures that would help make hunting easer for all.

Adam

"I know those soft hands," Igri laughed as he blindly searched for the holder to put away his paintbrush. He gently touched the hands of the human covering his eyes from behind.

The Festival of the Moon had ended a few hours ago and it was deathly quiet in Eden. Igri was about to complete his newest creature in the Tower of Arsinor. Azrael shined some of his yellowish glow in Igri's direction.

"Eve, my dear, let's have a look at you!" the old man said.

Eve waved Adam over to join them and planted herself before Igri with the assurance of a young princess.

"How did you know it was me?"

"I am the one who created you! None of God's other creatures has skin as soft and beautiful as yours."

She smiled, somewhat embarrassed, and hugged the old man.

"Well now, you have been gone for two weeks. Tell me, child, where have you two been?"

As Eve excitedly told Igri of her experiences at the glassy sea with the magnificent crimson-red sunsets, Adam glanced around in awe as he walked over to them.

He had never seen the inside of the Tower of Arsinor before.

He slowly made his way over to Igri's drafting table, which stood opposite from the entrance.

The walls reminded him of the study in the Glass Palace, except that these were rounded. And instead of books, small glass jars containing the Essences of Life filled the curved shelves perfectly crafted to fit the walls. A staircase wound along the wall to the top on four separate columns, each adorned with golden angelic runes.

To the right of the table that Igri used to paint his creations stood a giant board on which he drew rough sketches of his new designs.

Igri approached Adam with outstretched arms. Eve followed him.

"Look at you, Adam! You look like as if you have recovered well."

Adam was carrying a small package wrapped in fur. He handed it to Eve before tightly wrapping his arms around Igri. Several tears of joy rolled down his cheeks.

"I missed you!" he cried. "You were right. There are plenty of other wonders to discover beyond the Palace Gardens. Thank you for telling me."

"I have already been told that the two of you experienced many things out there," the old man replied with a laugh, stepping away from Adam's embrace.

He gently placed his hand on Eve's stomach as a faint smile spread over his face.

"But I promise you, the greatest wonder of all still lies ahead!"

He winked at Eve as he spoke.

Adam and Eve had no idea what he was talking about. They glanced at one another puzzled before beginning to laugh.

Eve unwrapped the fur-covered package. Inside were a few black pieces of fruit in the shape of large eggs, each with a rough peel.

"Look what we found," said Eve with a gleam in her eyes, holding up the fruit for the old man to see.

Igri took the fruit with a wary look.

"Tell me, you have not eaten of this fruit, have you?"

"No," said Adam. "It was too tough, and we had nothing to cut it with."

"Ahhhh, excellent. Then there is nothing to worry about."

"Why? Is the fruit poisonous?" asked Eve.

"This fruit was not made to be eaten. It has a different purpose," answered Igri, nodding to Adam.

"What purpose would that be?" Eve inquired.

"I already know this forbidden fruit from the Festival of the Moon," Adam said to Eve.

"Forbidden fruit? So no one is allowed to eat it?"

"It is forbidden for the fruit to touch the ground," said Igri.

"But why?"

Adam shrugged his shoulders, looking questioningly at Igri. Igri glanced over at Azrael, who had been silently following the conversation.

"Well," the angel began, "when the Festival of the Moon was reorganized following the Rebellion, there were a number of angels who did not take the athletic part of the Festival very seriously. In response, Igri created the fruit and I invented a legend to explain it. According to that legend, the moment the fruit touches the ground, the fall of all angels will commence."

"Fall of the angels?"

"It is merely a story," Azrael said with a laugh. "But only the four of us in this room, and of course the Father, know that.

Every angel fears the fall. And every one of us would give his life to keep any of the others from meeting this fate. Therefore, the Festival of the Moon is now taken extremely seriously; it provides each of us with strength."

As Azrael spoke, Eve walked slowly around the table to get a look at the board where Igri drew his rough sketches.

Her happy face gave way to a frightened look.

"What is this?"

"This is my latest creation. No need to be afraid," he said reassuringly.

"Such cold eyes. Such menacing teeth. Why are you creating such a terrifying being?" Eve asked.

"You still haven't heard? We created many, many more humans while you were away. Now we need more creatures, even bigger than before, to ensure that all of them have enough to eat. Aside from this, I was asked by a number of angels to create a few animals that were also more dangerous, so as to make the Festival a bit more challenging again. When I set about my work, I used some of the Essences from the previous Creation."

Adam found himself also growing curious. Was Igri talking about the very same Creation that he had ultimately destroyed? He glanced at the board. On it was a giant serpent with jaws gaping menacingly.

The next morning, Eve roused Adam from his sleep.

"Come on, let's go visit the Maze of Animals. I want to see the new creature!"

The day's first rays of sun had already struck the marble floor in the Throne Room as the two started off for the wooded path.

Ahead in the Maze, all was still asleep. The pair crept from glass case to glass case in search of the serpent. It was still very dark, and there was no trace of the Guardian Angels who normally helped to light the room.

"Over here, Adam! I found it!"

The young man tiptoed over to a large case perched atop a narrow pedestal at the edge of the building, close to the glass wall.

Adam recalled his first visit to the Maze and his episode with the narrow pedestals. He cautioned Eve to be careful. This case was three times as large as the other cases, and the young snake had already grown to an impressive size for its age. The animal lay motionless in its container.

"What do you think? How big will it be when it's fully grown?" Adam asked.

Eve shrugged her shoulders.

"What I'd rather know is: What does it eat?"

From the fur-wrapped package she had brought along, Eve took one small piece of forbidden fruit. She opened the glass case and dropped the fruit inside.

"Are you crazy? No one's allowed to eat the fruit!"

"The fruit isn't allowed to touch the ground. I'd like to see what happens when the animal eats the fruit. If nothing happens to it, then nothing will happen to us either!"

"But the fruit is way too big for the snake, and the peel is much too hard."

"Wait—something's happening!"

Wide-eyed, the two watched the snake as it slowly began to move. It took a few minutes for the snake to slither around the fruit and enclose it with its body. Then, the snake opened its jaws and swallowed up the fruit in one bite, without chewing at all.

"That's incredible!" said Eve astonished. "It just swallowed the thing whole!"

"There's no way we could do that," Adam said.

The snake slowly made its way towards the opening of the glass case. Adam marveled at the visible bump in the snake's otherwise slender body.

"We're home again, you know. I brought us something to cut it with," Eve said to him as she pulled out a second piece of forbidden fruit and cut it in two.

"What do you think? You want to try a piece too?" she asked Adam, offering him one of the halves. Juice seeped out of the fruit.

He said nothing as he took the piece from her hand.

"Let's do it together on the count of three," she said as she began to count:

"One ..."

They each held their halves in front of their mouths.

"Two ..."

Adam closed his eyes and opened wide. The snake locked its eyes on the fruit in Adam's hand, flicking its forked tongue.

"Three!"

At lighting speed, the snake bolted out of open case and snapped at the fruit in Adam's hand. Startled, Adam reflexively pulled his hand away, cutting it on the snake's sharp fangs in the process. Eve let out a shrill cry of terror and recoiled. As she lurched backwards, she bumped into a glass case containing a small monkey. The case began to tip. Like dominoes, the falling case crashed into two others, one holding insects and another with a tiny black kitten.

The noise woke all of the other animals, who then began to screech and hiss in a panic.

Eve sat crying on the floor amidst the shards of glass and all the insects and pieces of forbidden fruit.

"We have to tell the Father about this!" she sobbed.

"It's no big deal," Adam reassured her. "There are a couple of empty cases in the back. Here, help me pick up all the animals."

Eve scrambled to her feet and grabbed an empty case, while Adam closed the case that held the snake.

"Eve? Something's not right," he said with a tinge of fear in his voice.

She could only muster a questioning look as she stood in place holding the empty case.

The snake's case was closed, but Adam's hand remained wrapped around the handle. He looked as if he were falling over in slow motion.

"Adam? Are you ok?"

"My hands!" he screamed frantically. "Eve, help me! I can't move my hands, and now I don't have any feeling in my legs!"

Adam toppled over together with the large glass case, which smashed against the building's glass wall leading to the outside. The facade shattered. With a flip, the little monkey that was still running free sprang out of the building.

The kitten, too, was poised to escape. But Eve was quicker and trapped it in the glass case she had picked up moments before.

She turned to Adam and asked "What happened to you?"

Adam could hear the words, but he had no feeling in his mouth and began to pass out.

Some time later, he awoke. He was seated on the ground, propped up against the timber framework in front of the now-destroyed glass wall. Eve was busy trying to gather the rest of the insects crawling around on the floor. She looked at him without saying anything, visibly worried. It was clear to both of them that the situation had gotten out of control.

"What happened? "How long was I asleep?" Adam asked.

"I'm not sure. Breakfast is probably over by now," she said as she caught the last insect trying to crawl away. "I'm almost done. We have to tell the Father!"

Adam nodded in agreement and was relieved to see that he could once again feel his legs. He gingerly attempt to stand up.

"Adam? What happened?" a familiar voice asked him from behind.

Adam turned around. Standing outside before the shattered glass facade, a few yards away from Adam, was Igri, who looked worried.

"We're sorry! We really are!" Adam said as he broke into tears.

He glanced over at Eve, who simply stared—wide-eyed and stiff with fear—past Igri's head.

Adam turned back towards Igri, but what he saw startled him and he choked on his words. Trembling with fear, he pointed at something behind the old man. Igri turned around and dropped his stick to the ground, paralyzed with shock.

A giant ape, standing roughly seven yards tall, had planted itself behind Igri. With a balled fist, the animal smashed Igri into the ground like a hammer pounding a nail.

Eve shrieked in panic, inadvertently drawing the ape's attention inside the glass maze.

The creature was much too large to fit in the building.

Instead, the ape reached its arms through the shattered glass facade, blindly feeling around and knocking over a number of other cases in the process. Panicked, the now-free animals fled out of the building. Some were crushed by the ape, but most managed to escape.

Leaning against each other, Adam and Eve found their way to the back of a now completely destroyed Maze of Animals—out of reach of the giant ape, but right into the trap.

Michael

Word of the incident had not yet reached the Palace Gardens as the sun stood at the day's peak. It was a marvelous, hot summer day without a cloud in the sky.

"Adam and Eve returned last night," reported Azrael to the Lord. "They will soon have a child, though they still do not realize it."

"And how could they?" the Father said with a laugh. "No human has ever given birth to a child before. How is Igri coming along with the new creature?"

"It received the breath of life last night. I believe it will fulfill its purpose."

The Father nodded in satisfaction. He then turned to Michael who was silently following behind them.

"How is your brother faring?"

"He has not left the Lake of Fire. It appears that he is afraid. Day in and day out, he implores me to call a few Guardian Angels off of him and assign them to Adam and Eve.

"And what do you make of that?"

"Lord, it is not my prerogative to have opinions. You command, and I execute."

"Michael: No one else has spent as much time with Lucifer as you. If there is no other way, then I command you to tell me the truth. What do you think? Is it a trick?"

"At first, I believed it was," Michael answered. "Lucifer revels in being worshiped. But he has been begging me on his knees, and I believe that he is truly afraid. He swore to me that he would not leave the Lake of Fire without an explicit order, and over the past few days, I have witnessed nothing that would cause me to doubt his words."

All of a sudden, Michael's face grew very solemn. Without being ordered to do so, he turned away and started for the northwest corner of the Glass Palace with a focused look. The Father watched him, surprised that Michael no longer seemed interested in hearing His response.

"Michael? Is everything all right?" asked Azrael, staring in a bewilderment at the ledge of the Glass Palace, where nothing seemed to be amiss.

"I ... I am not sure," Michael stammered before racing over to the other side of the Palace through the passage beneath the balcony.

Azrael and the Father quietly exchanged a questioning glance.

"What have you seen?"

"It moved fast!"

"What did?"

"A huge shadow. I don't know!"

Suddenly, there was a scream from the Throne Room, followed by an aggressive growl and the sound of breaking glass.

Michael ran and positioned himself protectively in front of the Father, with both weapons drawn. The three stood a few yards away from the West Wall of the Palace, their eyes fixed anxiously on the balcony above.

More shattered glass fell to the marble floor, likely from the glass door leading to the balcony.

The other angels present stopped talking and likewise glanced nervously up at the balcony. Even Mu'rok had interrupted his meditation. With a fierce look, he watched the balcony above as he sharpened his spear.

Suddenly an oversized black cat leaped down from the balcony with a menacing roar. Michael pulled the Father with him as he dove to the ground. Azrael wavered, and remained paralyzed with shock as the cat bore its razor-sharp claws and raked the left half of his face. Azrael cried out in pain as he fell to the floor.

Michael pounced on the angry animal. There wasn't enough time to locate his weapons, as the beast grew larger with each additional second in the hot noonday sun. He seized the animal's two front legs and fought for his life.

Before he knew it, his back was pressed against the Palace wall. He could feel the strength draining out of his arms.

But then the giant cat let out a sharp yelp, followed by the sound of wood hitting metal. Mu'rok had thrown his spear square through the middle of the animal's back, its tip halted by Michael's armor.

"What is happening?" the Archangel panted as he shoved the lifeless animal off of him. The cat had grown to a height of over five yards.

The Father checked on Azrael. None of the angels dared to speak. The shock was still too great.

"My Lord, my Lord—the animals have escaped!" a voice cried down from above. It was Gabriel, gasping for breath as he landed.

"Father: The humans are in danger. The Northwest Settlements are already under attack!"

"What has happened?" the Father asked, exasperated.

"We do not know. But whatever it was, it happened hours ago."

Michael looked up at that sun.

"My God! We must do something. Immediately!"

The Father quickly glanced over to Mu'rok and nodded. Mu'rok pulled his spear out of the dead animal's back and let out an incomprehensible, ear-splitting battle cry that elicited a response from other Turonakki in the forests.

"That will not be enough, Father!" interjected Michael.

"Hundreds of little animals may have already grown into murderous beasts by now. As long as the sun allows them to grow faster than us, I fear that the humans have no chance of survival!"

"The Tower!" cried Azrael with a wheeze as he climbed to his feet.

"That is entirely out of the question," said the Father. "The humans would be separated from us forever!"

"But they have one another!" exclaimed Michael. "We do not have enough information about everything that is happening. Perhaps there is a way to reverse the process once things are safe again. One thing is certain, though: If we do nothing, we will see the end of humanity. Father, please! Give the command!" Michael urged as he retrieved his weapons, sheathing them on his belt.

"I can activate the Tower. Five strokes should be enough" volunteered Azrael.

"No!" cried the Father, grabbing Azrael's hand to keep him from leaving. He stood up and stared at the group.

Every face was full of trepidation; all eyes were tensely fixed on the Lord as they waited receive their command.

"Michael, you and Mu'rok will activate the Tower. You will find Eve's rib on the third floor. Mu'rok's is on the thirteenth. Five strokes! You must not fail!"

Michael rapped his chest with a balled fist, signaling his acceptance.

"Mu'rok, look after the humans. Show them how to survive. Guard them with your life, and obey them as you obey me!"

Mu'rok nodded before sprinting off in the direction of the Tower.

"Azrael, fly to the Lake of Fire as quickly as you can."

"Father?"

"We need Lucifer and the Guardian Angels for this battle. Everyone else: Protect the humans. Save them at all cost. Be prepared to give your life for theirs if it should come to that."

The angels struck their chest with a balled fist and fanned out in different directions.

"What shall You do, Father?" asked Azrael.

A tear rolled down the Lord's cheek.

"I shall search for Adam and Eve. For they will soon be all alone, and they will not know why. There is so much that I would like to tell them, and ... I hope that I still have enough time to quell some of their fear."

With that, the Father headed off for the Maze.

Michael flew to the Tower. Everywhere he looked, he saw angels and Turonakki embroiled in raging battles with giant creature.

But it was not his task to assist them in battle; his job was to end the chaos and restore balance.

He landed at the foot of the Tower of Arsinor and entered. Mu'rok had already reached the Tower and located Eve's rib. Michael found the Turonakko rib and flew to the top of the Tower as Mu'rok followed him on the staircase.

At the top of the Tower was a giant platform made of glass, at the center of which stood the Bell of Time, a bowl gong resting on three pedestals decorated with runes. Michael opened the seven seals and, together with Mu'rok, lifted the heavy lid off of the bowl.

He could see the Essence of Time, a sort of fog that radiated a bright white light. Michael tossed the two ribs into the bowl, and the Essence began to bubble. As he and Mu'rok began to heave the lid back in place, they were hindered by a pack of giant wolves that had followed and now encircled them. The wolves snarled and barked at them threateningly.

Michael drew his weapons and began his attack.

The wolves grew noticeably with each passing second in the hot midday sun. With a precise blow, he managed to knock one of the wolves off the platform.

Mu'rok, who like a monkey had the ability to coordinate his hand and feet separately, parried the attacks with his spear at lightning speed, masterfully dodging the fangs of the lunging wolves in what looked like an elegant dance.

Even so, the situation grew increasingly perilous. The size of the wolves had already surpassed what the angels could handle.

Michael had dropped his short sword at the edge of the platform and now stood with his back pressed against the Bell of Time. With both hands, he grabbed the wolf's muzzle and pressed it shut. The wolf scraped its claws furiously on Michael's armor. A second wolf leapt at Michael from the side, sinking its teeth into Michael's right forearm as he screamed in pain.

Meanwhile, Mu'rok had recovered Michael's short sword, which he promptly used to slice the tail off the wolf whose snout Michael had a hold of. With a howl, the injured animal backed away from the angel and pounced on the Turonakko.

There was no chance for Mu'rok to evade the attack, and the two went sailing off the platform into the abyss below. Michael could hear them continue their bitter fight as they plunged nearly 1,000 feet to the ground. Roughly halfway down, Mu'rok was able to jam Michael's sword into the rock wall, arresting his fall in dramatic fashion.

The wolf engaged with Michael at the top of the tower was now so large and powerful that it had no difficulty ripping the angel's forearm off.

Blood gushed into the bowl gong. The white fog turned a reddish hue and began to seethe ominously.

"No!" Michael groaned. "This was not the plan!"

The wolf howled as it was joined by five more giant wolves, all growing larger and stronger with each new second.

They snarled at Michael as they encircled him.

Michael closed his eyes in preparation for a final prayer.

"Forgive me, Lord! I have failed."

Just then, Michael heard the familiar sound of steel, accompanied by the squeal of death coming from one of the wolves. Astonished, he opened his eyes. Lucifer had appeared out of nowhere and slain the biggest wolf of the pack with one chop from his two-handed sword. A second wolf sprang to attack him. Lucifer, turning to gain momentum, cut the oncoming wolf in half in mid-leap.

Two more wolves pounced upon Lucifer from behind, sinking their teeth into his shoulders. The black angel thrust his sword into the corpse of his first victim as razor-sharp claws emerged from his fingers. Scratching the eyes out of the wolf clinging to his right shoulder, he snatched the other wolf and tossed him off the platform.

Lucifer reached for his sword—which immediately burst into red-hot flames from the handle to the tip—erupted in a deafening and terrifying roar, and trained his dark red glowing eyes on the remaining wolves.

His crimson angelic glow was so intense that it outshone even the light from the hot midday sun.

Despite their superior size and strength, the wolves halted their attack.

"Kill them, brother" Michael cried to Lucifer. "They are too dangerous to left alive!"

Lucifer did as he was commanded.

"It is good to see you finally submit to the Lord's will again."

Lucifer snorted as he slid the gong's lid back on and closed the seven seals.

"Hah! The Lord's will," he snapped at Michael disdainfully. "I lowered myself, begged you to keep this exact thing from happening! But you refused to listen. The forbidden fruit touched the ground. The Master of Creation was killed—by the hand of his own creation!"

"What?" said Michael, the fear and panic visibly spreading across his face.

"No part of what has happened today was ever planned!"

A horn sounded in the distance.

"Go, Lucifer. They need you. I will finish what needs to be done here."

"You fought well today, brother."

With those words, Morningstar took flight in the direction of the horn.

Michael crawled over to the giant mallet, which he tied tightly to his right upper arm. With all the strength he had left, he pulled himself up and swung the mallet against the Bell. What followed was a bright and warm ringing that could be heard all way to the Glass Palace.

The Father

Meanwhile, the Father had reached the destroyed Maze of Animals. In front of the building's entrance He came upon what remained of His oldest friend. In tears, He retrieved Igri's walking stick and called for Adam and Eve. There was no answer.

He looked around and discovered their footprints leading away from the building and deeper into the forest. It looked like they had been followed by something large. He followed the tracks, calling their names again and again.

A few yards ahead, He found the corpse of a giant ape with Michael's short sword stuck in its back. How did this get here? The Bell of Time had yet to ring. Had the white angel failed in his mission? Worried, the Father gazed in the direction of the Tower.

Cracking sounds coming from the undergrowth brought His mind back to Adam and Eve. He called for them again.

"Adam? Eve? Why are you hiding from me?"

No reply. A few yards further, He came upon a naked and wounded Mu'rok sitting against a tree. A number of Turonakki bodies lay lifelessly around him, their corpses still warm.

Mu'rok had likely dealt the beast the deciding blow just moments before.

The Father gently laid His hand on the wounded Turonakko. The wounds healed instantaneously.

Suddenly, He heard soft steps swiftly moving away from Him. He turned around and called once more for Adam and Eve. The steps fell silent.

All of a sudden, the first bright ring from the Bell of Time sounded. The Father panicked. Only four more rings until He would be separated from His favorite creatures for a long, long time. He stood still and raised His hands. He knew that Adam and Eve could hear and see Him. It was no use to keep on following them.

"Adam—What has happened?"

"It was Eve!" came his response. "She wanted to eat from the forbidden fruit!"

The second stroke sounded in the distance.

A tear rolled down the Father's cheek. What should He tell them? There was so much to say, but assigning the blame was not on that list.

He thought of the child that Eve was carrying. No human had ever given birth to a child before. He would have enjoyed being present for the event.

He thought about the pains of birth, and about how terribly confused and afraid she would feel in that moment.

"Eve, in pain you shall bring forth your children."

The third stroke sounded!

The Father spoke faster and faster, growing increasingly frantic. He had no time to carefully consider his words or explain things in detail.

"You will always feel drawn to your husband, but you shall submit to him!"

After all, Adam had already spent a few summer more in Eden, and had been instructed by Michael and the Turonakki.

There was the fourth stroke!

"Adam, you shall now be the master. Take care of your family, your brothers and sisters. From now on, you will need to work hard to feed everyone ..."

The Father was interrupted by a massive shock wave. He glanced over at the Tower in panic.

The fifth and final stroke did not sound.

"Adam?"

The two young humans emerged from their hiding spot and approached the Father together.

When they stopped directly in front of Him, they appeared not to see Him. Their worried eyes looked right through where His body should have been.

"Adam? Eve? I love you! I will find a way to unite us again!" he called as he broke out into tears.

Adam and Eve showed no response.

"What was that?" asked Eve.

Adam moved a few steps forward, passing through the Father as if He were a ghost. There was fear in Adam's eyes as he looked around. A little black kitten came running towards him through the woods.

Adam noticed that the rays of sun poking through the trees no longer caused the animal to grow larger. He looked at the dead Turonakki surrounding Mu'rok. There were no angels to be seen in the sky.

A crisp wind blew in his face.

He turned around, walked back to Eve, and answered her with a distraught look in his eyes:

"We have been punished."

The Fallen One

"And so it began ..."

The gleam from the metal in the creature's trembling hands had almost entirely waned. The letters of the final words were faint and barely legible.

Wheezing, the Fallen One dragged himself to the simmering shoreline and held the piece of metal to a flame with a deep reddish hue. The metal gradually began to glow red-hot again.

" ... the misunderstanding of sin! From that day forward, the humans tried to atone for their guilt. Guilt the Lord had refused to assign to them for even a single second!"

The piece of metal was now fully recharged and gave off a dark red glow in the hand of the Fallen One. He looked it over for a moment, lost in thought. He could see the reflection of his light blue eyes in the metal's smooth surface. But what was that? For a moment, it appeared that his eyes were crimson red!

Frightened, he jumped to his feet. His writing utensil slipped out of his fingers and landed on the ground next to the journal.

He slowly sat down again, opening the book to the next empty page.

"The humans and the Turonakki could neither hear nor see the Lord and His angels. At that time, we did not yet understand why. We could only agree that something had once again gone terribly wrong with the Tower.

Michael had disappeared."

The creature paused for a few seconds.

"Lucifer reported the unplanned mixing of the Essence of Time with the angel's blood. This combination would have unforeseeable consequences that not even Morningstar could conceive of. Not until the events at the Tower of Arsinor did we begin to grasp its far-reaching impact.

About the Author

Sven Majunke was born in Cottbus, Germany on May 20, 1983.

At the age of 17, he moved to the German city of Esslingen, where he completed an apprenticeship in mechatronics.

During this period, Majunke also began to explore Christianity and other religions.

In July of 2015, he discovered his flair for writing and embarked on his first literary work:

"The Rulers of Eden: Fall of Angels"

FSC
www.fsc.org
MIX
Papier | Fördert
gute Waldnutzung
FSC® C083411

Zeitfracht Medien GmbH
Ferdinand-Jühlke-Straße 7
99095 Erfurt, Deutschland
produktsicherheit@kolibri360.de